Hidden Emotions :
The Unknown Darkness

Vol. II

Poetry

Dedicated to the past

Because you keep coming back

Angelina Valencia

When I was l was little
I picked up a flower
and put it in a vase.
After a few days, it died.
I asked my mom why
and she said: "You can't force
a flower to thrive somewhere
it doesn't belong to."

And now I have realized that
people are like that too.

-   S.T.

Table of Contents

Hidden Emotions :
The Unknown Darkness

Vol. II

Angelina Valencia

Battle Wounds

I feel alone in places I shouldn't be
Like the walls close in on me
These tears in my eyes make it harder to see
I can't control my body from my anxiety
These negative thoughts — maybe I should
agree
I keep spending all my time even when I know
it's not free
But that's okay because I know I'm dying
quietly
I sit in these corners listening to my thoughts
privately
It's crazy because my heart tells me to love me
entirely
And that only I carry the key
To the only door that holds my happiness
guaranteed
But I can't help but wonder what's really
behind that door
Could it be someone I can finally hold?
Or will it be the darkness asking for another
war?
I keep asking please, I don't want this
anymore

But no one seems to listen to what I'm asking
for
No one seems to care, they just choose to
ignore
Maybe that's why every day I feel sore
From when everything would beat me to the
floor
How many times have I lost? Is anyone
keeping score?
Don't worry I know it's just like before
I've opened back up the battle wounds I've
tried not to restore

So is the world

Stop telling me I'm changing
Maybe it's because I'm growing older
Or maybe it has to do with
Peoples heart getting colder

I'm sorry I can't control
Everything that goes wrong around me
I shouldn't have to worry
About the people who surround me

I shouldn't have to be afraid
Of every step I take out of the door
Like something will steal my life
Then just leave me on the floor

So please stop saying *you're changing*
It's only my emotions being hurled
But who cares if I'm changing
So is the rest of the world

I care for so many people
        yet half of them want to die
why is it that

        nobody wants to stay

                    -    a.v.

I'm not letting you go

You say you don't know how you cry
Or how you still have tears
And these dreams that haunt you
They're bigger than your fears

You keep searching in hopes
For your pain there's a cure
But with the world that we live in
You won't find any here

Don't push me away
Don't tell me to leave
I know you want to be alone
But I know I'm the one you need

You're going to get through this
You're not doing this alone
I'm always going to be here for you
I'm not letting you go

Me or you

It's like you don't hear me
Like there's an invisible wall
I tried to climb over it but you didn't help me
Instead you just watched me fall

I'm screaming out for help to you
But it's like it's your ears you cover
I'm crying for you on one side
You're laughing on the other

Do you even care?
Like really, be honest
If you tell me *I love you*
Is that a promise?

I just want to know that you actually care
This wall I can't get through
Would you let me in
If it came down to me or you

The dark

I love being in the dark
It feels like it's where I belong
I can enjoy the silence
Or I can play my favorite song

There's something about the dark
The voices are louder in my mind
But I let them hold the microphone
And I leave my wall behind

There's a twist in my chest
But I swear it's all okay
My body isnt used to my guard being down
It's used to me throwing my emotions away

Just leave me in the dark
It's where I let myself go
The only difference is
No one will ever know

you promised you would stay
    but it feels like you're never here

       -   a.v.

What can I do

What can I do
You're on the other side of the screen
You tell me that you're sad
But what if it's worse than it seems

What if you tell me you're fighting through it
But really you're still crying
What if you tell me you're okay
But really you were lying

What if you tell me you had the best day ever
But really it was the worse
Something broke on the inside
But you don't tell me that you're hurt

Just what if you're not okay
You tell me something other than what you
feel
I could just be overthinking
But just tell me what is real

Angelina Valencia

Forbidden love

I want to kiss their lips
I want to hold their hand
But I'm prevented from doing so
Because you say I can't

I'm stuck in the middle
Loving them is exciting to me
But you prevent me from being happy
Because you don't think it's meant to be

Why can't you see that they make me smile?
They make my heart skip a beat
But of course you can't see that
It's like you don't know me

Allow me to want them
Because push comes to shove
Allow me to be happy
Because it shouldn't be forbidden love

It's not easy to forget

It's easy to remember
Not easy to forget
It's easy to remember
Everything you regret

You can't say that it's easy
All the memories can erase
Because in the back of your mind
There's always going to be space

The blurry vision of the future
The pain from the past
It's never going away
It's always coming back

It's hard to remember
Because you want to leave it behind
So no, it's not easy to forget
It's easy to press rewind

I'm okay

I'm okay, I'm okay, I'm okay
When will it come true?
Will I always be broken?
Will I always be bruised?

I'm fine, I'm fine, I'm fine
Is this even right to say?
I feel like everyone says this
Whenever they're not okay

I'm good, I'm good, I'm good
What does this even mean?
Is it an answer between bad and great
Or an answer that's our routine

Why do we say these things?
Is it a way to deny?
Will these ever be true?
Or will they always be a lie?

Who would've known
that making myself happy
doesn't matter to you

                    -    a.v.

Angelina Valencia

I'm letting go

A few months ago I lost you
I thought I never would
I've tried to move on
But yet I never could

I lost you suddenly
My heart wasn't ready
These pieces that you broke
I try and hold them steady

But now is the time
Now is the day
I let myself cry
As I stand by your grave

I will say one last goodbye
I will let my grief show
But this is the last time
Because I'm letting go

There's not enough words
    or there's not enough paper

             -    a.v.

Angelina Valencia

Don't tell me you're okay

Stop telling them you're okay
Stop telling yourself a lie
You know you struggle to live
You know you hate to cry

Even I know you're not fine
So don't tell me you're okay
You just had the worst breakdown
And that happened just today

There's nothing wrong with being hurt
There's nothing wrong with crying
There's nothing wrong with feeling lonely
There's something wrong with lying

Tell yourself you're not okay
Let yourself cry it out
Don't let it take over you
But don't let yourself go without

The mirror

I am home
And I don't mean under a roof
I have found myself
And I even have proof

There was nothing there before
Every time I looked in the mirror
There wasn't eyes, not a nose
Not a shadow not a figure

I couldn't see myself
I could find my true self
I couldn't see in any reflection
And nobody bothered to help

But now because of this person
I found love not fear
So when I look in the mirror
I am here

It takes months
        even years
to fix a broken heart

and yet it takes seconds
to break my heart —

        again

                    -    a.v.

Be careful

You said be careful who I choose
Be careful how I live
You said be careful how I love
Or I'll have nothing else to give

You said be careful where you go
Be careful where you stay
You said be careful who you trust
Because of the games they play

You said be careful what I watch
Be careful what you believe
Be careful what people tell you
Not everything is as it seems

You said be careful of all these
You could lose everything you own
But you see, I've got nothing to lose
Because of you I've been alone

I lost count

I've seen it all from the start
I can see it in your eyes
You're okay one second
But I know inside you've died

You can lift your head up
Even when it's heavy to hold
But your bones have cracked
Your body is turning cold

Yet you laugh with the same energy
You talk with the same tune
You smile the same warmth
You act the best of what's you

And yet after all these things that you hide
I was still able to see
I lost count of how many times
You've died in front of me

Down here

Down here it is dark
With a ladder I cannot climb
I can see the light above me
But a way out I cannot find

Help me when I need it
I'm reaching out my hand
But no one helps me get up
As if the darkness is what I am

I no longer belong here
I want to be free like those birds
But when I call out from down here
I'm never being heard

This ladder is my way out
But what if I don't want to go
Maybe the light is a dangerous place
Only the darkness is my home

I wish you didn't judge me
     before you even knew me

                    -    a.v.

Let me be free

This is something I have to do
Something I have to learn
For the good or bad
Making the decision is my turn

I don't want to lose you as a family
To lose you at all
But it's time I live my life
Just let me rise or fall

Please don't convince me otherwise
I promise I thought this through
I am happy where I am
And no, I promise I'm not replacing you

Please be happy for me
Please don't be sad, mad, or disappointed in
me
I promise when I say he's such a good person
Please let me be free

I wish I knew I felt so down today

- a.v.

It's not fun

You think this is fun?
Because it's not even a bit
I don't like sleepless nights
I don't want to go through this

It's not fun crying at midnight
With no one at my side
I would reach for someone's hand
But my emotions tend to hide

I'm sorry for worrying
You're the one person I don't want to lose
It's actually my biggest fear
Please don't let that be you

I try my best to hold it in
I try my best not to overthink
But sometimes I can't help it
I'm slowly drowning underneath

Fear...

it breaks me down

- a.v.

It's happening again

It's happening again
The heavy feeling
The weight in my chest
The burning sensation is revealing

I thought I was over it
I thought I was done
I thought it wasn't coming back
But yet the past still wants to have fun

When will it end
I don't want this anymore
Please don't put me through this again
I thought I beat you before

I guess it never leaves
It burns a hole in my heart
Maybe that's how it should be
Watch me go back to falling apart

Why

Why does *I'm sorry* exist
It's not always real
Why do emotions exist
When we never know what we feel

Why are promises made
If they're always going to be broken
Why do we have to explain ourselves
Not everything can be spoken

We "fix" cracks in things
We cover holes in walls
But they will always remain there
We just can't see it at all

So why do we pretend
To be something we are not
When in the end
The truth is always caught

I'm not

I'm not scared
I'm not lost
I'm not hurt
You're not the reason I fought

I'm not concerned
I'm not broken
I have everything in control
I don't hold on to the promise spoken

I'm not mad
I'm not nervous
I don't cry anymore
I still feel like I have a purpose

Did I convince you enough?
Do you care that I tried?
All that I said above...
See how easy it is to lie?

Angelina Valencia

Why do you want to see me
        You've hurt me enough

                    -    a.v.

Slow down please

Slow down please
There's only so much I can take
You want me to keep standing
Then don't continue to break

It's okay don't worry
I know what they did to you
But don't mess up your life
And end up taking the wrong path too

This isn't who you are
It's not all about drugs
I'm worried about you
Stop rejecting people's hugs

You're better than this
I know everything for you is tough
But don't choose to go down a cliff
Because not all the time can you climb back
up

I've got a lot to say

I've got a lot to say
But yet no words come out
I'm trying to understand
I'm trying to focus what this is about

I've got a lot to do
But my body doesn't want to move
It wont let me help you out
It's forcing me to watch the wrong path you
choose

I've got a lot to fight
I thought I was strong enough
But sometimes the strongest crew
Aren't the ones that can stay up

I've got a lot to say
But you don't want to listen
Maybe it's not my words
You're missing

And here I thought
    everything was okay

           -    a.v.

I've never cried so much
like I did today

                    -   a.v.

It went away

It went away
I never thought it would
But it has decided to leave
I never thought it could

I've learned to laugh
I've learned to smile
I learned all the things
That didn't exist for awhile

It's like living another life
I can say I'm actually free
Because just not that long ago
I was never the real me

But yet here I am
Free of it all
You'll never look down on me again
Because you'll never see me fall

I felt afraid today
    and I don't know why

           -   a.v.

Mental Abuse

Okay I'm going to be completely honest
So here's the truth
It'll help explain all
And help you understand too

The number one thing is
I'm a person to apologize a lot
Everyone tells me to stop doing that
Even though I know it's not my fault

I also break down randomly
But I've learned to manage alone
The bathroom was my hiding spot
Even when no one was home

I also never accept compliments
I just find it hard to be true
But just understand
These are signs of mental abuse

Why do you feel the need to hurt me?

What's the point?

- a.v.

I shouldn't be afraid to see you

or better yet

I shouldn't be afraid of you

- a.v.

Please wake me up

Please wake me up
Please open my eyes
Stop surrounding me with what I have
Everyone around me wants to die

Keep the good things I have
Take the bad away
Why are you going to hand me those
That don't even bother to stay

Help me out here
I'm lost in the crowd
Am I a good person
Is anyone proud?

Please wake me up
This is the worst dream
Why tell me it's all okay
When life isn't what it seems

Just lie to me

Just lie to me
Trust me its best for both of us
You honestly think it's better
Because it's not something to discuss

You're not welcome back in my life
I let you go a long time ago
So please do what is best
It's best if you never show

I might be a little aggressive
But you messed up my life
You said one thing
But stabbed my back with a knife

Please, I'm finally happy
I don't want the haunted past
I let that all go
Your memories are last

Angelina Valencia

Take a while

How am I supposed to feel
Fear takes over my control
One minute I feel happy
The next I don't feel whole

It's a lack of communication
To be honest I feel lost
I'm not even sure how to speak
I feel like its a dead end I crossed

It's messing with my head
We both feel the same
The only difference is
It's in so many different ways

I'm sorry, I really am
I didn't mean to hurt you
But I'm happy where I'm at
It's just going to take me a while too

I won't know

I have six main people in my life
Half want to die
So stop asking every day
Why do you want to cry

It's because I care too much
And I love to hard
I can't just sit there and say
I'm going to put down my guard

I need you
I need them
They're what makes up the flower
I'm just the stem

It won't make sense
Without it I can't
Be myself anymore
Because I won't know who I am

I don't know if I should give up

or let myself get hurt

- a.v.

I don't know what to say

I don't know what to say
Maybe I'll know later
But if I did
I'd run out of paper

I feel low
And don't ask why
Everything happens for a reason
But I shouldn't cry

Or maybe I'm wrong
But what if I'm not
What if all the emotions
Were once found but lost

Help me figure it out
Can't do this alone
I need someone to care
Someone who is my home

Angelina Valencia

One or the other

Mind is blank
Emotions are real
It's almost like no thinking
But yet it's everything we feel

We lose interest
In the most important things
Sometimes we lose ourselves
In the lost and found it'll be

Then there are days
It's the happiest we've ever been
Our smile is wider than ever
We really take these days in

These are two sides
It's either one or the other
But this is only temporary
It doesn't last forever

Maybe my fears are meant to be faced—

who will I lose first?

- a.v.

Angelina Valencia

Unhappiness

I wonder what it'll take
For you just to realize
What you actually did
It was never you that kept me alive

You tell me I'm always happy
It's different when I'm alone
Yes I'm always positive
But I never felt at home

I taught myself to be happy
I taught myself to be okay
It's almost like hiding
My emotions are put away

You'll never know the real me
Even though you're supposed to
I wonder if my unhappiness
Was all because of you

Mold me

I heard you were looking
For something different
Should I change my ways?
To where you wouldn't miss it

I heard you wanted
Your certain shape and form
A person's nature
To be perfect in your own

I heard you needed
Someone everyone wants
Attention you crave
But the love is thrown and tossed

Change me to the person you want
Shape me the way you please
No matter my appearance
I'll always be me

My last

What if it was my last day
What if it was my last words
What if it was my last laugh
What if I were to never return

What if it was my last move
What if it was my last step
What if it was my last hug
What if I don't know what's next

What if it was my last song
What if it was my last writing
What if it was my last poem
What if I found nothing worth fighting

What if was my last thought
What if it was my last text
What if I closed my eyes
And took my last breath

If I put my life in your hands

Would you save it?
Hide it?
Destroy it?
Or love it?

- a.v.

Angelina Valencia

I can't help it

What did I do
To deserve this
Am I caring too much?
I didn't ask to reserve this

Why does everyone want to leave
Nobody bothers to stay
I should be used to it by now
But yet it hits me everyday

I'm sorry but I can't help it
When it's my biggest fear
Should I stop holding them close?
Should I stop letting them near?

Will it be so wrong
To not want to care anymore?
If everything will be okay again
Should I just not be there anymore?

Can I be alone?

Can I be alone
Just for a few
Lock me in a room
The dark is nothing new

I feel a little lost right now
Can I be alone?
Let me find myself
I'm somewhere in this home

Is it so wrong to feel off?
Like something is wrong
Can I go cry?
Be weak instead of strong?

Can I just be alone?
Please?
This world isn't broken —
It's me

Is this what we're doing now?
    Pretending?

With just a smile?

                    -    a.v.

He left.
She left.
They left.

Now you.

I'm close to giving up

-   a.v.

It's still taking time for me

You broke a promise

- a.v.

I'm reminded

Why did it have to be me
Why have I been chosen
I don't deserve this
I just want to live my moments

Instead it's hard for me to stand
I enjoy the dark
I take in the silence
Because you picked me apart

The little things remind me
Of all the bad things
I want to be okay
But your so called "affection" is really
haunting me

Someone told me 'you work so hard
I hope your parents treated you right'
And there again I'm reminded
Of all the things I have to fight

I don't want to lose you too

-    a.v.

I exist
I live
I breathe
I'm here

to you I'm not

- a.v.

What?

no, I'm fine

- a.v.

It's easy for me
    just to wipe my tears
      and smile

- a.v.

Don't forget about me

Sorry for crying last night
I just felt distant
Like you don't want me anymore
I'm sorry I just miss it

Don't pull away from me
Don't forget about me
Don't forget I'm here
I love you so don't doubt me

I just don't want wanna lose you
I don't want us to give up
You're all I see in my future
I want it to be just us

I love you so much
Please don't give up on me
If you were to ever leave
I don't know who I'll be

I.Hate.My.Head.

- a.v.

I'm tired.

- a.v.

Hold up my pieces

I was right again
My head got the best of me
But it was warning me
Before pain got the rest of me

I felt the distant
I felt different energy
I felt like something was wrong
And now I have painful memories

I shouldn't be sad
You're doing this to focus on yourself
It just hits different
What will I do with myself

I was only happy because of you
I'm better because of you
I feel like I just failed
Who's gonna hold up my pieces too

Why am I always right?

Why does my mind have to overthink to the
point where I'm proven right

again

- a.v.

and here I thought we'd be forever

\-   a.v.

And just like that

you erased me

- a.v.

It's okay
I'll be okay

eventually

    -   a.v.

Book three coming soon!